Also by Rachael Reed

Codefendant
Codefendant
Once a Cheater
Once a Cheater
Passport Bro
What Happens in Prison
Preference
Sprinkle Sprinkle
Championship Bad
Street Exodus
Street Exodus
Street Royalty
Pawns of Power
SIS
Cartel Bloodline
Get Money Girls
Skip the Games
Til Death Do Us Part
Backpage Hustle
Link in Bio

Link In Bio

Rachael Reed
©2024

Link in Bio

By Rachael Reed

Copyright © 2024 by Rachael Reed

Chapter 1: The Façade

Mari Monroe, known to millions as the glamorous social media influencer, stared at her reflection in the mirror. Her makeup was flawless, her hair perfectly styled, and her outfit on point. But behind the carefully crafted facade, she was a mess. The vibrant woman her followers adored was a shell, struggling to hold herself together after her fiancé, Justin, had ditched her a year ago.

"Alright, y'all, get ready with me," Mari said, forcing a bright smile as she hit record on her phone. She moved through her makeup routine with practiced ease, chatting about the latest trends and upcoming collaborations. Her followers loved her energy, her confidence, her seemingly perfect life. They had no idea that she cried herself to sleep most nights, haunted by memories of what should have been.

Mari's phone buzzed with notifications as she posted the video. She glanced at the screen, her smile faltering. The date loomed closer—what would have been her wedding day. She needed to get away, to escape the constant reminders of her failed relationship and the pressure to maintain her online persona. South Florida seemed like the perfect destination. Sunshine, beaches, and a chance to find herself again.

She announced her spontaneous trip to her followers, making it sound like a carefree adventure. "Gonna catch some sun and clear my mind! Stay tuned for beach pics and travel vlogs!" The comments flooded in, filled with excitement and envy. Her fans couldn't wait to see her living it up in paradise.

Behind the scenes, Mari booked a last-minute flight and packed her bags. She needed this getaway more than her followers could ever understand. The pressure to be perfect, to always appear happy and successful, was suffocating. She longed for a break from the constant performance, a chance to breathe and figure out who she was without the filters and hashtags.

The airport was chaotic, a stark contrast to the calm facade Mari projected online. She slipped on her oversized sunglasses and pulled her hat low, hoping to avoid recognition. She couldn't handle the fake smiles and forced small talk today. She just wanted to get on that plane and leave everything behind.

As the plane took off, Mari stared out the window, watching the city shrink below her. She felt a strange mix of relief and anxiety. This trip was a gamble, a desperate attempt to find herself in the midst of the storm that had become her life. But she had to try. She couldn't keep living a lie, pretending to be okay when she was anything but.

Landing in South Florida, Mari was hit by a wave of heat and humidity. She welcomed the change, hoping it would help melt away some of her stress. She checked into a chic beachfront hotel, her room offering a stunning view of the ocean. She could almost feel her worries starting to wash away.

That evening, Mari decided to explore the area. She wandered through the bustling streets, taking in the sights and sounds of South Florida. The energy was different here, raw and real. She felt a flicker of something she hadn't felt in a long time—excitement. Maybe this trip would be the fresh start she needed.

She found a cozy beach bar and decided to stop in for a drink. The place was lively, filled with locals and tourists mingling and laughing. Mari ordered a cocktail, hoping the alcohol would help take the edge off her nerves. She needed to relax, to let go of the stress and sadness that clung to her like a second skin.

"Hey, you're Mari Monroe, right?" a voice interrupted her thoughts. She turned to see a young woman with a wide smile and starstruck eyes.

"Yeah, that's me," Mari replied, forcing a smile.

"I love your videos! You're such an inspiration," the woman gushed. "Can I get a selfie with you?"

"Of course," Mari said, slipping into her influencer mode. She posed for the photo, her smile bright and perfect. But inside, she felt a pang of sadness. Even here, miles away from her usual life, she couldn't escape the facade.

After the woman left, Mari sighed and sipped her drink. She needed to find a way to break free from this cycle, to discover who she was beyond the screens and filters. She was lost in thought when a shadow fell across her table.

"Mind if I join you?" a deep voice asked.

Mari looked up to see a tall, dark-skinned man with a confident swagger. He had a dangerous edge to him, something that both intrigued and scared her. "Sure, why not," she said, curious about this stranger.

"I'm Jace," he said, sitting down and giving her a charming smile. "And you are?"

"Mari," she replied, feeling a strange connection to him.

As they talked, Mari felt a spark of something she hadn't felt in a long time. Jace was different from anyone she'd met before. He had an air of mystery and danger, and he seemed genuinely interested in her. For the first time in a long while, she felt seen, not as an influencer, but as a person.

The evening stretched on, filled with laughter and deep conversation. Mari found herself opening up to Jace in a way she hadn't with anyone since Justin. There was something about him that made her feel safe, even as she sensed the darkness in his world.

As the night drew to a close, Jace walked her back to her hotel. "I had a great time tonight," he said, his voice soft and sincere.

"Me too," Mari replied, surprised by how much she meant it.

"Let's do this again," Jace suggested, his eyes holding a promise of something more.

"Yeah, I'd like that," Mari said, feeling a flutter of excitement.

As she watched him walk away, Mari felt a mix of emotions. She was drawn to Jace, but she knew he came with complications. Still, she couldn't deny the connection they shared. Maybe this stormy surprise was exactly what she needed to find herself again.

Mari entered her hotel room, her mind buzzing with thoughts of Jace. She knew she was in for a wild ride, but for the first time in a long time, she felt alive. The storm had brought her to this place, and she was ready to see where it would take her.

Chapter 2: Hurricane Chaos

Mari lay in bed, the distant roar of the approaching hurricane echoing through her hotel room. She stared at the ceiling, replaying the events of the past few hours. She had come to South Florida for peace and solitude, but the sudden storm and her unexpected encounter with Jace had turned everything upside down.

The wind howled outside, rattling the windows. Mari glanced at her phone. Social media was buzzing with news of the hurricane, her followers bombarding her with messages. She could almost hear their voices: "Stay safe, girl!" "Can't wait to see your hurricane selfies!" She rolled her eyes, tossing the phone aside. The facade was becoming harder to maintain.

She sighed, deciding she needed a distraction. Grabbing her umbrella, she headed downstairs to the hotel lobby. As she walked through the deserted halls, she felt the oppressive weight of the storm pressing down on her. The once lively hotel was now a ghost town, with guests either evacuated or hunkered down in their rooms.

Mari reached the lobby and found Jace leaning against the reception desk, talking to the hotel manager. His presence was a stark contrast to the chaos around them. Calm and composed, he looked up and flashed her a smile.

"Hey there, city girl. Decided to brave the storm?" he asked, his tone teasing.

Mari forced a smile. "Yeah, I figured I'd see what the fuss was about."

The hotel manager, a petite woman with frazzled hair, nodded towards Mari. "We're setting up a makeshift shelter in the ballroom. It's safer there, away from the windows."

Jace nodded. "Good idea. Come on, Mari. Let's get you settled."

As they walked towards the ballroom, Mari felt a mix of anxiety and curiosity. Jace had an air of mystery that both intrigued and unsettled her. He wasn't just another guest; there was something dangerous about him. She could feel it in the way he carried himself, the way he spoke.

Inside the ballroom, hotel staff were setting up cots and distributing blankets. The atmosphere was tense, with guests huddled together, their eyes wide with fear. Mari took a cot near the back, away from the crowd. Jace followed, sitting down next to her.

"You okay?" he asked, his voice softer now, almost concerned.

Mari shrugged. "I guess. This wasn't exactly the trip I had in mind."

Jace chuckled. "Life's funny that way. Sometimes it throws a hurricane at you."

Mari looked at him, studying his face. There was a hardness in his eyes, a story she wanted to unravel. "What about you? What brings you here?"

Jace's smile faded, replaced by a more serious expression. "Business," he said, his tone clipped. "But enough about that. Tell me about you. Why South Florida?"

Mari hesitated. She wasn't used to talking about herself, not the real her. But there was something about Jace that made her want to open up. "I needed a break. My life's been... complicated lately."

Jace nodded, as if he understood more than he let on. "Well, you picked one hell of a break. But hey, maybe this storm will blow away all the crap and give you a fresh start."

Mari smiled, despite herself. "Yeah, maybe."

As the night wore on, the hurricane's fury intensified. The ballroom shook with each gust of wind, the lights flickering ominously. Mari and Jace talked about everything and nothing, finding comfort in each other's company. It was strange, this connection with a stranger, but it felt real in a way her online interactions never did.

Suddenly, a loud crash echoed through the ballroom as a window shattered, sending glass flying. Screams erupted, and the hotel staff rushed to contain the damage. Mari's heart raced as she crouched down, feeling Jace's hand on her shoulder.

"It's okay, I got you," he whispered, pulling her closer.

The chaos around them seemed to blur, and for a moment, all that mattered was the safety she felt in Jace's presence. The storm raged on, but Mari found herself strangely calm. Maybe it was the adrenaline, or maybe it was Jace, but she felt a spark of something she hadn't felt in a long time—hope.

As dawn broke, the hurricane began to weaken, leaving a trail of destruction in its wake. The guests slowly emerged from their makeshift shelter, surveying the damage with weary eyes. Mari stood up, stretching her stiff limbs, and looked at Jace.

"What now?" she asked, her voice hoarse.

Jace smiled, that dangerous edge returning to his eyes. "Now, we rebuild. And who knows, maybe we find something worth holding onto."

Mari nodded, feeling a sense of determination rise within her. The storm had tested her, but it hadn't broken her. With Jace by her side, she was ready to face whatever came next. The chaos of the hurricane had brought them together, and now, as the skies cleared, they had a chance to find their own path.

Chapter 3: Temporary Sanctuary

The ballroom was eerily quiet, except for the howling wind and the occasional crash of debris against the hotel walls. Mari sat on her cot, glancing around at the other guests who were equally tense and uneasy. She couldn't shake the feeling of vulnerability, being trapped in a strange place during a hurricane. The anxiety gnawed at her, but there was something else too—a spark of curiosity about the man who had become her unexpected protector.

Jace sat across from her, his eyes scanning the room, ever alert. He had a presence about him that was both reassuring and intimidating. Mari couldn't quite put her finger on it, but there was an air of authority in the way he carried himself, a confidence that suggested he was used to being in control.

"You holding up okay?" Jace asked, his voice cutting through the storm's din.

"Yeah, as well as I can, I guess," Mari replied, forcing a smile. "This isn't exactly what I had in mind for a vacation."

Jace chuckled. "Life's full of surprises. Sometimes you just gotta roll with the punches."

Mari nodded, studying him. "What about you? You seem pretty calm, considering."

Jace shrugged, a faint smirk playing on his lips. "I've seen worse. This? This is just another day."

The way he said it sent a chill down Mari's spine. She leaned in closer, lowering her voice. "What do you do, Jace? I mean, really."

Jace's eyes flicked to hers, and for a moment, she thought he wouldn't answer. Then he leaned back, crossing his arms. "Let's just say I handle business. Not the kind you'd find in an office."

Mari's curiosity was piqued. "And what kind of business is that?"

Jace's smile widened. "The kind that stays off social media. The kind that gets you into places like this with no questions asked."

Mari shivered, partly from the cold and partly from the implication of his words. There was danger in his world, real danger, and she was teetering on the edge of it. But instead of fear, she felt a strange excitement. She had been living a lie for so long, pretending to be someone she wasn't. Maybe a dose of reality, however gritty, was exactly what she needed.

As the hours passed, the tension in the ballroom grew thicker. The storm outside showed no signs of letting up, and the guests huddled together, whispering and casting anxious glances at the windows. Jace, however, remained unperturbed, his calm demeanor a stark contrast to the chaos around them.

"You ever been in a situation like this before?" Mari asked, trying to break the silence.

Jace nodded. "More times than I can count. You learn to adapt, stay sharp. Fear'll get you killed quicker than a bullet."

His words hung in the air, a grim reminder of the reality he lived in. Mari found herself wanting to know more, to understand this man who seemed so unflinching in the face of danger.

"What's it like? Your life, I mean," she asked, her curiosity getting the better of her.

Jace's expression darkened slightly. "It ain't glamorous, that's for sure. It's a lot of late nights, a lot of looking over your shoulder. But it's the life I chose. And it's the life that's kept me alive."

Mari nodded slowly, absorbing his words. She had spent so much time crafting a perfect image online, but here was a man who lived with raw honesty, who faced the darkness head-on. It was a stark contrast to her world of filters and followers.

"Why'd you come here?" Jace asked, turning the question back on her.

Mari hesitated, then sighed. "I needed to get away. My fiancé... well, ex-fiancé, left me. I've been pretending everything's fine, but it's not. I'm tired of pretending."

Jace's eyes softened, and he leaned forward. "I get that. Sometimes you gotta strip away the bullshit and see what's real. You're here now, and you're dealing with it. That takes guts."

Mari smiled, a genuine smile this time. "Thanks. I guess we all have our storms to weather."

The hours dragged on, and the storm outside began to show signs of weakening. The guests in the ballroom started to relax, the immediate threat seeming to pass. Mari and Jace continued to talk, their conversations ranging from the mundane to the profound. She learned about his past, the struggles he faced, and the choices he made. In turn, she shared her own story, the pressures of her online persona, and the emptiness she felt inside.

By the time the wind had died down and the rain turned to a light drizzle, Mari felt a connection to Jace she hadn't expected. There was a raw honesty between them, born out of the shared experience of the storm.

As dawn broke, the hotel staff began to usher the guests back to their rooms, assessing the damage and planning the cleanup. Jace stood up, stretching his limbs, and offered Mari a hand.

"Come on, let's get you back to your room," he said.

Mari took his hand, feeling a warmth spread through her. "Thanks, Jace. For everything."

He shrugged, but his eyes held a hint of warmth. "Anytime. And hey, maybe when this is all over, we can grab a drink or something."

Mari nodded, her heart skipping a beat. "I'd like that."

As they walked back through the now quiet halls, Mari couldn't help but feel a sense of anticipation. The storm had brought chaos, but it had also brought Jace into her life. And she had a feeling this was just the beginning of a new, unexpected journey.

Chapter 4: Dangerous Attraction

The hurricane had passed, leaving behind a trail of destruction and a strange calm. The sun broke through the clouds, casting a deceptive light on the chaos below. Mari sat by the window of her hotel room, staring out at the broken branches and scattered debris. Her mind, however, was far from the storm's aftermath. It was fixated on Jace.

In the days following the hurricane, Mari and Jace had spent a lot of time together. The forced proximity during the storm had created a bond, and now, as the skies cleared, that bond seemed to strengthen. Jace had a magnetic pull, an allure that Mari found impossible to resist. His world was dangerous, filled with shadows and secrets, but there was something intoxicating about the way he navigated it with confidence and control.

"Yo, Mari, you good?" Jace's voice broke through her thoughts. He stood in the doorway, his presence commanding the small space.

Mari turned, offering him a small smile. "Yeah, just thinking."

"Thinking 'bout what?" He walked over, his gaze intense and probing.

She hesitated, unsure how to articulate the turmoil inside her. "About this... about us."

Jace smirked, a knowing glint in his eye. "Us, huh? Didn't know there was an 'us.'"

Mari blushed, feeling a mix of embarrassment and excitement. "You know what I mean. This thing between us. It's dangerous."

Jace sat down next to her, his expression serious now. "Life's dangerous, Mari. But sometimes you gotta take risks."

She sighed, looking back out the window. "It's just... your world, it's so different from mine. I'm not sure I can handle it."

He reached out, his fingers brushing hers. "You think my world is different? Trust me, the streets ain't so far from where you come from. We all just tryna survive."

His words struck a chord, and Mari found herself nodding. "Maybe. But it's more than that, Jace. I don't want to just survive. I want to live. I want to be free."

Jace leaned in closer, his voice a low murmur. "Freedom ain't free, Mari. You gotta fight for it. And sometimes, you gotta get your hands dirty."

Her heart pounded as he spoke. There was truth in his words, a raw honesty that she couldn't deny. Despite the danger, despite the risks, she felt herself being pulled deeper into his orbit.

The next few days were a whirlwind. Jace took Mari around the city, showing her the reality of his world. They visited rundown neighborhoods where poverty and crime were rampant. Jace introduced her to people who lived on the edge, their lives a constant struggle against the odds. It was a stark contrast to the curated perfection of her social media life, and it was both terrifying and exhilarating.

One evening, as they walked through a dimly lit alley, Jace stopped, turning to face her. "Mari, you sure you wanna be part of this? My life ain't easy. It ain't safe."

She looked into his eyes, seeing the vulnerability beneath the tough exterior. "I don't know, Jace. But I know I can't pretend anymore. I need something real."

He nodded, his jaw set in determination. "Then let's make it real."

Their relationship intensified. The line between attraction and danger blurred as Mari found herself more and more entangled in Jace's life. The passion between them was undeniable, a fire that burned bright and hot. But with it came the constant threat of violence, the ever-present danger that lurked in the shadows.

One night, as they lay in bed, Mari traced the scars on Jace's chest with her fingers. "How do you do it, Jace? How do you live like this?"

He looked at her, his eyes dark and serious. "You get used to it. You learn to fight, to protect what's yours. And you don't let fear control you."

She nodded, feeling a surge of resolve. "I want to be strong like you. I want to fight."

Jace smiled, a rare softness in his expression. "You already are, Mari. You just gotta believe it."

Their nights were filled with whispered confessions and shared dreams, their days with the harsh reality of Jace's world. Mari struggled to adapt, to find her place in the chaos. But with each passing day, she felt herself growing stronger, more resilient.

But the danger was always there, a dark cloud that loomed over them. One evening, as they walked through a bustling market, Jace suddenly tensed. "We gotta go. Now."

Mari's heart raced as she followed him, weaving through the crowd. "What's wrong?"

"Trouble," he muttered, his eyes scanning the area. "Just stay close."

They ducked into an alley, the tension thick between them. Mari could feel the fear creeping in, but she pushed it down, focusing on Jace. He was her anchor, her guide through the storm.

As they waited, hiding in the shadows, Mari realized something. Despite the danger, despite the fear, she felt alive. For the first time in a long time, she felt truly alive.

Chapter 5: A Taste of the Underworld

The sun was setting, casting long shadows over the gritty streets of South Florida. Mari, once the epitome of social media perfection, found herself in a place far removed from the pristine images on her Instagram feed. She was with Jace, her enigmatic protector and guide into a world she never imagined she'd see.

"Yo, Mari, you ready for this?" Jace asked, his tone casual but his eyes serious.

Mari nodded, her heart pounding with a mix of fear and excitement. "Yeah, let's do it."

Jace led her through the maze of narrow alleys and rundown buildings. The air was thick with the smell of smoke and sweat, a stark contrast to the sanitized world of luxury hotels and pristine beaches she was used to. Mari felt out of place, yet strangely alive, as if she was finally experiencing something real.

They stopped at a run down warehouse, the walls covered in graffiti and the windows barred. Jace knocked on the door in a specific pattern, and it swung open to reveal a large man with a scowl on his face.

"This is Mari," Jace said, introducing her with a nod. "She's with me."

The man eyed Mari suspiciously before stepping aside to let them in. Inside, the warehouse was a hive of activity. People moved about, handling large packages and counting stacks of money. The air was charged with tension, and Mari could feel the weight of their stares as she walked by.

"Welcome to the real South Florida," Jace said, his voice low. "This is where the magic happens."

Mari looked around, taking in the chaotic scene. She had seen movies about the underworld, but nothing could have prepared her for the reality. It was gritty, dangerous, and raw. The people here lived by a different set of rules, where survival depended on strength and loyalty.

Jace guided her to a small office in the back, where a man with a scarred face sat behind a desk. He looked up as they entered, his eyes narrowing.

"Jace," he greeted, his voice rough. "Who's this?"

"Mari," Jace replied. "She's with me."

The man's gaze shifted to Mari, appraising her. "You sure about that?"

Jace nodded. "Yeah, I'm sure."

The man shrugged and returned to his paperwork. "Just keep her out of trouble."

Jace led Mari back out into the main area. "That was Rico. He's one of my main guys. Runs the operations here."

Mari nodded, trying to process everything she was seeing. "Is this what you do? Deal drugs?"

Jace glanced at her, his expression unreadable. "It's part of it. But it's more than that. It's about control, about power. You learn to navigate this world, or you get swallowed by it."

They left the warehouse and continued their tour of the underworld. Jace introduced her to more of his associates—tough, hardened men and women who looked at her with a mix of curiosity and suspicion. She could feel their judgment, their silent questions about why she was here.

As they walked, Jace explained the dynamics of his world. The rivalries, the alliances, the constant need to watch your back. It was a stark contrast to the life Mari had known, where her biggest concern was maintaining her online image.

At one point, they stopped at a street corner where a group of men were gathered. One of them stepped forward, a smug grin on his face.

"Jace, my man," he said, slapping Jace on the back. "Who's the pretty lady?"

"Mari," Jace replied, his tone cold. "She's with me."

The man looked Mari up and down, his grin widening. "Nice. Real nice. You sure she's cut out for this life?"

Jace's eyes hardened. "Don't worry about her. She's stronger than she looks."

Mari felt a surge of pride at his words, but also a flicker of fear. This was a dangerous world, and she was just starting to understand what it meant to be part of it.

As they walked away, Jace turned to her. "You okay?"

Mari nodded, though her mind was racing. "Yeah, just... it's a lot to take in."

"I know," Jace said, his voice softening. "But you wanted to see my world. Now you have."

They continued walking, the streets growing darker as night fell. The city seemed to change with the setting sun, becoming more sinister and alive. Mari's initial fear was giving way to a strange fascination. There was something intoxicating about the danger, about the raw reality of Jace's life.

They ended up at a small, dimly lit bar. Jace ordered drinks, and they sat in a corner booth, away from prying eyes. As they sipped their drinks, Mari couldn't help but ask the question that had been nagging at her.

"Why do you do it, Jace? Why live this life?"

Jace stared into his glass, his expression contemplative. "It's what I know. Grew up in it, learned to survive in it. It's not about choice anymore. It's about survival."

Mari nodded, understanding more than she ever had before. "But you could get out, couldn't you? Start fresh?"

Jace looked at her, a small smile playing on his lips. "Maybe. But it's not that simple. This life has a way of pulling you back in, no matter how far you try to run."

Mari reached across the table, taking his hand. "Maybe you just need a reason to leave."

Jace squeezed her hand, his eyes dark and intense. "Maybe."

The night wore on, and Mari felt the weight of her new reality settle in. She was in deep now, entangled in a world she barely understood. But as she sat there with Jace, she felt a strange sense of belonging. This was dangerous, yes, but it was also real. And for the first time in a long time, she felt truly alive.

Chapter 6: The Unraveling

Mari sat in front of her phone, her makeup immaculate, her hair perfectly styled, and her outfit curated to the last detail. She forced a smile and hit record. "Hey, guys! So today, I'm going to show you my latest makeup haul and give you some tips on how to stay fabulous even when you're traveling!" Her voice was bright and cheerful, but inside, she felt like she was falling apart.

As she went through the motions, she couldn't stop thinking about Jace. Her time with him had been intense, filled with danger and excitement. But it was worlds away from the pristine, polished life she projected online. The comments on her videos and posts were starting to reflect the growing dissonance.

"Girl, where you at? Your pics look hella different lately."

"Why you in South Florida? Everything okay?"

"Yo, who's that guy you were spotted with?"

Mari closed the app, her heart racing. The speculation and gossip were starting to surface. People were noticing the cracks in her facade. She could feel her carefully constructed online persona beginning to unravel, and it scared her.

Her phone buzzed with a call from Lila, her best friend and confidante. "Mari, what the hell is going on? Your followers are blowing up my DMs asking if you're okay. Are you?"

Mari sighed, rubbing her temples. "I'm fine, Lila. I just needed a break."

"A break? With some mystery guy in the middle of a hurricane? This isn't you."

"Maybe it is," Mari snapped, surprising herself with the vehemence in her voice. "Maybe I'm tired of pretending to be someone I'm not."

Lila was silent for a moment. "Who is he, Mari? Is he trouble?"

Mari hesitated. "His name's Jace. And yeah, he's trouble. But he's also real. He sees the real me, not just the online version."

"Be careful, Mari. I don't want to see you get hurt."

"I know. I will." She hung up, feeling a pang of guilt and confusion. Her life was spiraling out of control, and she didn't know how to stop it.

That evening, Mari met Jace at a dimly lit bar on the outskirts of town. The place was a far cry from the upscale venues she usually frequented, but it had a raw, gritty charm that she was starting to appreciate. Jace was leaning against the bar, talking to a man with a scar running down his cheek. He looked up as she approached, his eyes lighting up with a mix of warmth and concern.

"Hey, you good?" he asked, pulling her close.

"Yeah, just... dealing with some stuff," Mari replied, trying to push her worries aside. "Who's your friend?"

"This is Rico. We go way back," Jace said, introducing her to the scarred man.

Rico nodded, his gaze assessing. "So, this the girl you been talkin' about, Jace? She don't look like she belong in our world."

Mari bristled at the comment but held her tongue. Jace squeezed her hand, a silent reassurance. "She's tougher than she looks."

Rico shrugged, turning back to his drink. "We'll see about that."

As the night wore on, Mari found herself immersed in Jace's world. She met more of his associates, each with their own stories of survival and struggle. There was an unspoken code among them, a bond forged through shared experiences and mutual respect. It was a far cry from the superficial connections she had online, and she found herself drawn to it, despite the danger.

But as she got deeper, the lines between her two worlds began to blur. She struggled to maintain her online image while dealing with the harsh realities of Jace's life. The pressure was suffocating. She found herself constantly looking over her shoulder, wondering when her secrets would catch up to her.

One night, as she sat on Jace's couch, scrolling through her social media feed, she saw a post from a popular gossip site. "Influencer Mari

Monroe spotted with South Florida's notorious Jace. Trouble in paradise?" The post was accompanied by a grainy photo of them together, looking far too cozy for just friends.

Her heart sank. The facade was crumbling faster than she could manage. She felt exposed, vulnerable. Jace walked in, noticing her distress. "What's wrong?"

"Look," she said, showing him the post.

Jace frowned, reading the article. "So what? Let 'em talk. They don't know shit."

"But my followers... my image. This could ruin me," Mari said, her voice trembling.

Jace sat down beside her, taking her hand. "Mari, you gotta decide what's more important. Your image or your truth. You can't have both."

She knew he was right, but it didn't make the decision any easier. She had built her entire life around her online persona. Letting go of that felt like losing a part of herself. But at the same time, she was tired of the lies, the pretense.

That night, as she lay in Jace's arms, she made a decision. She would start being real, no matter the cost. She would show her followers the person she was becoming, the person she wanted to be. And if they couldn't accept that, then so be it. She was done living a lie.

Chapter 7: Secrets and Lies

Mari sat on Jace's couch, her heart pounding as she scrolled through the photos and articles she had found. Jace was in the kitchen, making coffee, oblivious to the storm brewing inside her. The more she learned about his past, the more conflicted she felt. She had known he was dangerous, but the full extent of his criminal activities was staggering.

"Yo, you want sugar in this?" Jace called out, his voice a comforting rumble despite the tension in the room.

"Yeah, sure," Mari replied absentmindedly, her eyes glued to the screen.

The articles detailed Jace's involvement in drug trafficking, violence, and a slew of other crimes. His enemies were numerous and ruthless, and Mari couldn't ignore the growing sense of dread in the pit of her stomach. She had thought she could handle his world, but now she wasn't so sure.

Jace walked over with two mugs, handing one to Mari before sitting down next to her. "What's got you so deep in thought?"

Mari hesitated, then turned the screen towards him. "This. All of this."

Jace's eyes darkened as he took in the images and headlines. "I told you my life ain't pretty."

"I know, but... it's more than that, Jace. This is serious. These people, they're dangerous."

He sighed, running a hand over his face. "Yeah, they are. But so am I."

"Is that supposed to make me feel better?" Mari snapped, her frustration boiling over.

Jace leaned closer, his gaze intense. "Look, I ain't gonna lie to you. My life is fucked up. But I'm doing what I gotta do to survive. To protect the people I care about."

Mari's anger softened slightly, but the fear remained. "And what about me, Jace? How do I fit into this?"

Jace reached out, cupping her face in his hands. "You fit, Mari. You fit because you're real. You're not just some fantasy. You're here, with me, in this mess. And I need you."

Mari felt a tear slip down her cheek. "But what if it gets worse? What if we can't handle it?"

"We'll handle it," Jace said firmly. "Together."

Their moment was interrupted by a loud bang at the door. Jace was on his feet in an instant, his hand reaching for the gun he kept hidden nearby. "Stay here," he ordered, his tone brooking no argument.

Mari's heart raced as she watched him approach the door. The fear was palpable, her mind racing with worst-case scenarios. She could hear muffled voices, angry and insistent. Then a scuffle, and the sound of something heavy hitting the floor.

Jace reappeared, his face a mask of fury. "Pack your stuff. We gotta go. Now."

"What? Why?" Mari asked, her voice trembling.

"Just do it!" Jace barked, his tone leaving no room for questions.

Mari scrambled to gather her things, her mind spinning. This was it. The danger she had feared was now at their doorstep. She had a choice to make: stay with Jace and face whatever came their way, or run back to her safe, lonely life.

As they hurried out of the apartment, Jace kept a firm grip on her hand, guiding her through the darkened streets. They moved quickly, keeping to the shadows, Jace's paranoia evident in every cautious glance.

"Where are we going?" Mari whispered, her voice barely audible over the pounding of her heart.

"Someplace safe," Jace replied, his eyes scanning their surroundings.

They reached an old, dilapidated building and slipped inside. Jace led her to a small room at the back, locking the door behind them. The room was bare, save for a mattress on the floor and a few scattered belongings. It was a far cry from the luxurious hotels Mari was used to, but it was their refuge for now.

Jace sat down heavily on the mattress, his shoulders slumped. "I'm sorry, Mari. I didn't want this for you."

Mari sat beside him, taking his hand in hers. "I knew what I was getting into. I chose this."

He looked at her, a mixture of gratitude and regret in his eyes. "You don't have to stay. You can leave, go back to your life. It's not too late."

Mari shook her head. "No, Jace. I can't go back to pretending. I want to be with you, even if it's dangerous. We'll figure this out together."

Jace pulled her into his arms, holding her tightly. "I promise I'll keep you safe."

The resolve in his voice was comforting, but Mari knew the road ahead would be anything but easy. They were in deep, and there was no turning back now.

As the night wore on, they talked about their next steps. Jace's enemies were closing in, and they needed a plan to stay ahead. Mari's fear was overshadowed by a fierce determination to stand by Jace, no matter the cost.

Chapter 8: The Escape Plan

Mari paced the small room, her mind racing as Jace sketched out his plan on a worn map spread across the floor. The dim light cast long shadows, adding to the tension that hung in the air. Every muscle in her body was taut with anxiety, but she was determined to see this through. She had chosen this path, and there was no turning back.

"Alright, so this is how it's gonna go down," Jace said, his voice low and steady. "We hit them where it hurts, right in their supply line. Without their product, they got nothing."

Mari nodded, trying to absorb the details. She had never been involved in anything like this, but the stakes were too high to back out now. "And you're sure this will work?"

Jace looked up, his eyes meeting hers with a fierce intensity. "It's risky, but it's our best shot. We take out their operation, and they'll be scrambling. It'll give us enough time to disappear."

She swallowed hard, the gravity of the situation sinking in. "What do you need me to do?"

Jace hesitated for a moment, then pointed to a section of the map. "You'll be our lookout. We need someone who can keep a low profile and watch for any signs of trouble. You think you can handle that?"

Mari squared her shoulders, determination hardening her resolve. "I can handle it."

The next few days were a blur of preparations. Jace's crew moved in and out of the safe house, each member focused on their role in the plan. Mari felt out of place at first, but as she got to know the people Jace trusted with his life, she began to feel a part of the team. They were rough around the edges, but they had a loyalty to Jace that ran deep.

"Yo, Mari," a gruff voice called out, snapping her out of her thoughts. She turned to see Rico, Jace's right-hand man, leaning against the doorframe. "You ready for this?"

Mari nodded, her stomach churning with a mix of fear and excitement. "Yeah, I'm ready."

Rico studied her for a moment, then nodded approvingly. "You got guts, I'll give you that. Just keep your head down and your eyes open. We can't afford any mistakes."

The night before the plan was set to go into action, Jace and Mari found a rare moment of quiet. They sat on the mattress, the weight of what they were about to do hanging heavy in the air.

"You scared?" Jace asked, his voice barely above a whisper.

Mari looked at him, seeing the vulnerability beneath his tough exterior. "Terrified. But I trust you."

He took her hand, squeezing it gently. "I won't let anything happen to you. I promise."

The day of the operation arrived, and the tension was palpable. Mari's role as the lookout meant she would be positioned on a rooftop across from the rival gang's warehouse. She had a clear view of the entrance and could signal to Jace if anything went wrong.

She climbed up to the rooftop, her heart pounding in her chest. The city sprawled out below her, a maze of streets and alleys that hid both danger and opportunity. She settled into her position, trying to steady her breathing.

Jace's voice crackled through the earpiece she wore. "You in position?"

"Yeah, I'm here," Mari replied, scanning the area. "All clear for now."

"Good. Keep your eyes peeled. We're moving in."

Mari watched as Jace and his crew approached the warehouse, their movements swift and precise. Her pulse quickened as she saw them slip inside, the tension ratcheting up with each passing second. She kept her gaze fixed on the entrance, ready to signal at the first sign of trouble.

Minutes felt like hours as she waited, her nerves stretched to the breaking point. The street below remained eerily quiet, the calm before the storm. Suddenly, movement caught her eye. A group of men appeared at the far end of the alley, heading towards the warehouse.

"Jace, we've got company," she whispered urgently into the earpiece. "About six guys, armed."

"Shit," Jace muttered. "Alright, sit tight. We're almost done here."

Mari's heart raced as she watched the men get closer. She could hear the muffled sounds of a struggle coming from inside the warehouse, and her mind raced with worst-case scenarios. She gripped the edge of the rooftop, her knuckles white.

The men reached the entrance and paused, seemingly unsure of what to do next. Mari took a deep breath, then pulled out the flare gun Jace had given her. It was a last resort, a signal for the crew to abort the mission if things went south.

Just as she was about to fire, the warehouse doors burst open. Jace and his crew emerged, dragging a few beaten and bloody men with them. The group at the entrance hesitated, clearly caught off guard by the sudden turn of events.

"Go, go, go!" Jace shouted, and his crew sprang into action, taking down the remaining threats with brutal efficiency.

Mari watched in awe and horror as the scene unfolded below her. The violence was quick and decisive, a stark reminder of the world she had stepped into. But it was also strangely exhilarating, a rush of adrenaline that left her breathless.

Within minutes, it was over. Jace looked up at her, a grim smile on his face. "We did it. Get down here."

Mari climbed down from the rooftop, her legs shaking as she made her way to Jace. He pulled her into a tight embrace, his relief palpable. "You were perfect," he murmured against her hair.

She held onto him, feeling the weight of the danger they had just faced together. "What now?"

"Now we get the hell out of here," Jace said, his voice filled with determination. "We got what we needed. It's time to disappear."

Chapter 9: The Heist

The night air was thick with tension as Jace and his crew prepared for the heist. They gathered in a rundown warehouse on the outskirts of the city, their faces grim and focused. The plan was simple but risky: hit their rivals hard and fast, taking out their supply line and securing their own safety. But in the world Jace navigated, nothing ever went according to plan.

"Alright, listen up," Jace said, his voice cutting through the murmur of whispered conversations. "This is it. We go in, we hit them quick, and we get out. No mistakes. No hesitations."

Mari stood off to the side, her heart pounding in her chest. She had insisted on being there, on seeing this through. She needed to prove to Jace, to herself, that she was committed. But now, as the reality of the situation set in, she couldn't ignore the fear gnawing at her gut.

Jace caught her eye, a silent question passing between them. She nodded, steeling herself for what was to come. He walked over, his expression softening slightly. "You good?"

"Yeah," she replied, her voice steadier than she felt. "Let's do this."

The crew moved out, slipping through the shadows like ghosts. Mari followed close behind Jace, her senses on high alert. They reached the rival gang's warehouse, a hulking structure surrounded by barbed wire and guarded by armed men. Jace signaled for everyone to take their positions.

"Rico, you and your boys take the east side," Jace ordered. "Mari, you're with me."

They crept towards the entrance, Mari's heart hammering in her chest. She kept her eyes peeled for any sign of trouble, her nerves stretched to the breaking point. Jace led the way, his movements smooth and controlled. He was in his element, and despite her fear, Mari couldn't help but admire his skill.

They reached the door, and Jace nodded to Mari. She took a deep breath and pushed it open, her adrenaline spiking as they slipped inside. The warehouse was dimly lit, stacks of crates and barrels casting long shadows across the floor.

"Stay close," Jace whispered, leading her through the maze of storage. "We need to find their stash and take it out."

They moved quickly, their footsteps echoing in the cavernous space. Mari's pulse quickened as they approached a group of men huddled around a table. Jace motioned for her to stay back, then crept closer, his gun at the ready.

The men looked up, surprise flashing across their faces. "What the fuck?" one of them exclaimed, reaching for his weapon.

Jace didn't hesitate. He fired a single shot, taking the man down. Chaos erupted as the others scrambled for cover, bullets flying in every direction. Mari ducked behind a crate, her heart in her throat.

Jace moved with lethal precision, taking out their opponents one by one. Mari watched in awe and horror, her fear giving way to a strange sense of exhilaration. She had never been this close to such violence, and it was both terrifying and intoxicating.

Suddenly, a hand grabbed her from behind, yanking her to her feet. She gasped, struggling against the iron grip. "Gotcha, bitch," a rough voice snarled in her ear.

Mari twisted, trying to break free, but the man was too strong. He dragged her towards the center of the room, his gun pressed to her temple. "Jace! Let her go, or she dies!"

Jace froze, his eyes locking onto Mari's captor. His face was a mask of fury and fear. "Let her go," he growled, his voice deadly calm.

"Drop your gun, and maybe I will," the man sneered.

Jace hesitated, his mind racing. He couldn't afford to lose Mari, but he couldn't let his guard down either. "Mari," he said, his voice steady. "Close your eyes."

She obeyed, her heart pounding. A gunshot rang out, and the man holding her went limp. She stumbled forward, her legs shaking, and Jace caught her, pulling her into his arms.

"You okay?" he asked, his voice rough with emotion.

Mari nodded, her breath coming in short gasps. "Yeah. I'm okay."

They didn't have time to linger. The rest of the crew had taken care of the remaining threats, and they needed to move fast. Jace led Mari to the stash, a hidden room filled with drugs and weapons. They set the charges, rigging the place to blow.

"Let's get the fuck outta here," Jace said, his grip on Mari's hand tight.

They ran, the adrenaline coursing through their veins. They burst out of the warehouse just as the first explosion rocked the building. Flames licked at the sky, and the ground shook beneath their feet. They didn't stop until they were far enough away, the sounds of destruction fading into the distance.

Jace pulled Mari close, his eyes searching hers. "You did good, Mari. You were brave."

She smiled, her heart swelling with a mix of pride and relief. "We did it."

But the victory was bittersweet. They had struck a blow against their enemies, but the cost had been high. Mari's life had been put in danger, and the reality of Jace's world had never been clearer.

Chapter 10: The Fallout

The sun barely peeked over the horizon as Mari and Jace stumbled into the safe house, exhausted and covered in grime. The adrenaline from the heist had long worn off, replaced by the harsh reality of what they had done. Jace's crew followed, a mix of triumphant and haunted expressions on their faces. They had pulled it off, but not without a cost.

Rico slumped against the wall, clutching his arm where a bullet had grazed him. "Shit, Jace. That was some crazy-ass shit. We lost Tino and Mike."

Jace's face hardened, the losses hitting him like a sledgehammer. "We knew the risks. Tino and Mike... they knew what they signed up for."

Mari watched the exchange, feeling a pang of guilt. She had seen the violence, felt the danger, but the reality of death was something else entirely. She moved to help Rico with his wound, trying to push down the nausea that threatened to overwhelm her.

As the crew settled, Jace pulled Mari aside. "We need to talk."

They stepped into a small, dimly lit room. Jace shut the door behind them, his expression unreadable. "What's wrong?" Mari asked, her voice trembling.

"What's wrong?" Jace echoed, his voice rising. "You almost got yourself killed back there, Mari. This ain't a game!"

"I know that!" Mari shot back, anger flaring. "Do you think I wanted to be in that situation? But I'm here, Jace. I'm trying to help."

"Help? You think this is help? You're a liability, Mari. You ain't built for this life."

The words stung, and tears welled up in Mari's eyes. "I chose to be here. I chose you. But if you think I'm just some helpless girl, maybe you don't know me at all."

Jace's face softened, and he took a deep breath. "Look, I just... I can't lose you, Mari. Not like this. This life, it's gonna tear us apart."

"Then let me in," she pleaded. "Let me be part of it. We can face it together."

He ran a hand through his hair, the tension evident in his posture. "It's not that simple. There are things you don't know, things you shouldn't know."

"Like what?" Mari demanded, stepping closer. "What are you hiding, Jace?"

He hesitated, and Mari could see the conflict in his eyes. "There's a lotta shit, Mari. Things I've done to survive. Things I ain't proud of. You deserve better than that."

"I deserve the truth," she said firmly. "Whatever it is, I want to know."

Jace sighed, looking away. "Alright. You wanna know the truth? Fine. I've killed people, Mari. Not just in self-defense, but because it was necessary. I've lied, cheated, and stolen to stay alive. And now, because of this heist, we're marked. The rival gang's gonna come for us, for you. This ain't over."

Mari's heart pounded in her chest. The weight of his words settled over her like a shroud. "I knew it was dangerous, but... damn, Jace. I didn't know it was this bad."

"That's why I wanted to keep you out of it," Jace said, his voice softer now. "I wanted to protect you."

She reached out, touching his face. "I don't need protection. I need you. All of you. We'll figure this out, Jace. Together."

He pulled her into his arms, holding her tightly. "I hope you're right."

The days that followed were a blur of tension and preparation. The crew fortified their hideout, anticipating retaliation from the rival gang. Mari found herself more involved than ever, helping where she could, learning the ropes of Jace's world. But the strain began to show, the stress of their situation taking its toll.

One evening, as they sat in the dimly lit living room, Mari confronted Jace again. "I've been hearing things. The crew, they're whispering. They don't trust me."

Jace's expression darkened. "They're just cautious. You're new to this. Give it time."

"Time? Jace, we might not have time. They think I'm a liability, and honestly, I can't blame them."

Jace's jaw clenched. "I'll handle it. They'll come around."

But the mistrust within the crew continued to grow. Rico, once somewhat supportive, now eyed Mari with suspicion. Tensions flared during meetings, with murmurs of betrayal and doubt.

One night, as they sat around the table planning their next move, Rico stood up, slamming his fist on the table. "We got a mole, Jace. Someone's been leaking info, and it's gotta be her."

Mari's eyes widened in shock. "What? That's insane! I've done nothing but try to help."

Rico glared at her. "Help? Ever since you showed up, shit's gone sideways. We're losing people, Jace. We can't afford any more risks."

Jace stood, his voice dangerously calm. "Rico, sit down. Mari ain't the problem. We got enemies on all sides. Blaming her ain't gonna fix that."

Rico reluctantly sat, but the tension remained thick. Mari felt the weight of their distrust, the precariousness of her position in this dangerous game.

Later, in the privacy of their room, Mari confronted Jace. "This isn't working, Jace. The crew doesn't trust me, and it's tearing us apart."

Jace looked weary, the burden of leadership heavy on his shoulders. "I know. But we gotta stay strong. We can't let them see us divided."

Mari nodded, but the doubt lingered. The fallout from the heist had exposed cracks in their foundation, and she wasn't sure how much longer they could hold on.

Chapter 11: Turning Point

Mari stood in front of the mirror, her reflection a stark contrast to the vibrant influencer her followers knew. Dark circles shadowed her eyes, and her expression was one of exhaustion and turmoil. She picked up her phone, the familiar weight of it both comforting and suffocating. The world she had created online felt like a distant dream now, a facade she could no longer maintain.

She glanced at the door, where Jace's silhouette lingered. His presence was a constant reminder of the life she had chosen, the dangers she had embraced. But now, as tensions within the crew grew and trust eroded, she knew she had to make a choice. With a heavy heart, she turned to face him.

"Jace," she began, her voice trembling, "I think it's time for me to go."

Jace's eyes narrowed, a mix of confusion and hurt flashing across his face. "What you talkin' 'bout, Mari?"

"I can't do this anymore," she admitted, tears welling up. "The danger, the mistrust... it's too much. I need to get back to my life, my followers."

Jace took a step closer, his expression hardening. "You think you can just walk away? After everything we've been through?"

Mari shook her head, wiping away a tear. "It's not that simple. I love you, Jace, but I can't keep living like this. I need to find myself again."

He looked away, his jaw clenched. "Fine. Do what you gotta do. But don't expect me to wait around."

With that, Mari packed her bags, the weight of her decision pressing down on her. She took one last look at Jace, his back turned, and walked out the door, feeling a part of her heart break with each step.

The flight back to her old life felt like an eternity. As the plane touched down, she was filled with a sense of dread. Her followers had no idea what she had been through, the darkness she had faced. She wasn't sure she could go back to the superficial world of likes and comments.

Mari stepped into her apartment, the familiar surroundings feeling foreign and cold. She took a deep breath and opened her laptop, logging into her social media accounts. The notifications flooded in, her followers eagerly awaiting her return.

"Hey, everyone! I'm back!" she typed, forcing a smile. "Missed you all so much."

The responses were immediate and overwhelming, her fans showering her with love and questions. But as she scrolled through the comments, she felt a growing sense of emptiness. The praise and admiration felt hollow, a stark contrast to the raw emotions she had experienced with Jace.

Days turned into weeks, and Mari struggled to reintegrate into her old world. She posted pictures and videos, attended events, and tried to maintain the vibrant persona her followers adored. But every night, as she lay in bed, the memories of South Florida haunted her. The adrenaline, the danger, the love she had felt for Jace – it was all too real to forget.

One evening, after a particularly exhausting day of filming, Mari sat on her balcony, staring out at the city lights. She thought about Jace, wondering what he was doing, if he was safe. The pain of their separation gnawed at her, and she felt a deep longing to be with him again.

Her phone buzzed, and she glanced at the screen. A message from Lila, her best friend, popped up. "Hey girl, saw your latest post. You okay? You seem... different."

Mari sighed, typing a quick response. "I'm fine, just a lot on my mind."

Lila's reply was almost immediate. "Wanna talk? I can come over."

Mari hesitated, then agreed. Maybe talking to Lila would help. She needed to unload the burden she was carrying, even if she couldn't share everything.

When Lila arrived, she hugged Mari tightly. "You look like you've been through hell."

Mari laughed bitterly. "You have no idea."

They sat down, and Mari recounted her time in South Florida, carefully omitting the most dangerous details. She talked about Jace, the intensity of their relationship, and the struggle to balance her old life with the new reality she had faced.

Lila listened, her expression a mix of concern and curiosity. "Mari, you went through all that and didn't tell me? Why?"

"I didn't want to worry you," Mari admitted. "And honestly, I didn't know how to explain it. It's like I've lived a whole different life."

Lila nodded. "Sounds like you have. But what now? Are you going back to him?"

Mari shook her head. "I don't know. Part of me wants to, but... I'm scared. Scared of what it means, scared of losing myself again."

Lila took her hand, squeezing it gently. "You need to do what's right for you. But if you love him, really love him, maybe it's worth the risk."

Mari looked out at the city again, her mind racing. She thought about the danger, the violence, the love she had felt for Jace. Could she really go back to that life? Could she leave her old world behind for good?

Chapter 12: A Call for Help

Mari was sitting in her pristine, stylish apartment, attempting to film another makeup tutorial. Her followers were growing restless with her lack of updates, and she needed to maintain her facade. But her mind kept drifting back to South Florida, to Jace. She missed him more than she cared to admit, and the emptiness gnawed at her.

Just as she was about to finish her video, her phone buzzed with a notification. She glanced at it, and her heart skipped a beat. It was a message from Jace.

"Need you. In trouble. Can't trust anyone else. Please."

Mari's breath caught in her throat. She re-read the message, her mind racing. She had tried to distance herself, to return to her old life, but this plea for help shattered any resolve she had. She couldn't turn her back on him, not now.

Without a second thought, she grabbed her phone and dialed his number. It rang twice before going to voicemail. "Jace, it's Mari. I got your message. I'm coming. Hold on."

She packed a bag quickly, throwing in essentials and a few changes of clothes. Her heart pounded as she booked a last-minute flight back to South Florida. She knew the risks, knew what she was walking back into, but she couldn't let fear stop her.

The flight was a blur. Mari's thoughts were consumed with worry for Jace. What kind of trouble was he in? Was he hurt? The anxiety gnawed at her, making the hours stretch endlessly. She tried to distract herself by scrolling through her social media, but it only reminded her of the hollow life she had been living.

When the plane landed, she felt a mixture of dread and determination. She was stepping back into a world of danger and uncertainty, but she couldn't stay away. Jace needed her, and she couldn't let him down.

She made her way to the address Jace had sent in a follow-up message. It was an old, rundown motel on the outskirts of town. The place reeked of desperation and decay, a stark contrast to her polished life. She hesitated for a moment, then steeled herself and knocked on the door.

It swung open to reveal Jace, his face bruised and battered. Relief and pain flashed in his eyes when he saw her. "Mari, you came."

She rushed to him, her hands gently touching his injuries. "What happened to you?"

Jace winced, stepping aside to let her in. "Got jumped. Rico betrayed me. Sold me out to the rivals."

Mari's blood ran cold. Rico had always been a wildcard, but this was worse than she imagined. "We need to get you out of here," she said, her voice trembling with urgency.

Jace shook his head, sitting down heavily on the bed. "No. They'll be looking for us. We gotta lay low, figure out our next move."

Mari knelt beside him, her heart breaking at the sight of his pain. "I'm not leaving you, Jace. We'll figure this out together."

He looked at her, a mix of gratitude and regret in his eyes. "I never wanted to drag you into this. You should've stayed away."

"Too late for that," Mari replied, her voice firm. "I'm here now. We're in this together."

The next few days were a whirlwind of tension and planning. Jace's injuries made it difficult for him to move, but Mari did her best to care for him. They strategized, trying to outmaneuver Rico and the rival gang. It was a dangerous game, one that required cunning and ruthlessness.

One evening, as they sat in the dimly lit motel room, Jace turned to Mari. "You know, you could still walk away. This life... it ain't for you."

Mari shook her head, her resolve unshakable. "I've made my choice, Jace. I'm not going anywhere."

He took her hand, his grip weak but determined. "You're braver than you know."

Mari smiled, but the worry never left her eyes. "We need a plan. A way to get out of this mess for good."

Jace nodded, his mind working despite the pain. "I got an idea. But it's risky. We need to hit them where it hurts. Take out Rico and the rival leaders. It's the only way to end this."

Mari's heart pounded. The plan was dangerous, but it might be their only shot. "Tell me what to do."

They spent the night mapping out their strategy, every detail critical to their survival. Mari's fear was overshadowed by her determination to see it through. She had come too far to back down now.

Chapter 13: The Rescue Mission

Mari crouched behind the dumpster, her heart pounding like a drum in her chest. The gritty alleyway was dimly lit, shadows dancing ominously as she waited for the signal. Jace's remaining allies, a ragtag group of hardened individuals, were scattered around her, their faces grim with determination.

"Alright, listen up," Jace whispered, wincing from the pain of his injuries. "This is it. Rico and his boys are holed up in that warehouse. We go in, get the drop on them, and take out anyone who stands in our way. No mercy."

The crew nodded, their eyes reflecting the dangerous reality of their world. Mari's hands trembled slightly, but she steadied herself. She was here to prove her loyalty, to show Jace and his crew that she was more than just a pretty face.

Jace turned to her, his gaze intense. "Mari, you stay close to me. No heroics, you hear?"

She nodded, swallowing her fear. "I got it, Jace. Let's do this."

They moved as one, slipping through the shadows towards the warehouse. The air was thick with tension, every sound amplified in the stillness of the night. Mari's pulse raced as they approached the entrance, her mind flashing back to the moments that had led her here.

Jace pushed the door open, the rusty hinges creaking loudly. They stepped inside, the darkness swallowing them whole. The warehouse was a labyrinth of crates and machinery, perfect for an ambush. Mari kept her eyes peeled, her senses heightened.

Suddenly, a figure lunged out from the shadows, aiming a gun at Jace. Mari reacted without thinking, shoving Jace aside and taking aim with her own weapon. The shot rang out, the man crumpling to the ground.

"Nice shot," Jace muttered, getting back to his feet. "But be careful."

They pressed on, the tension ratcheting up with each step. Voices echoed through the cavernous space, and they followed the sound, moving stealthily. Mari's heart pounded as they rounded a corner and came face-to-face with Rico and his gang.

"Well, well," Rico sneered, his gun trained on Jace. "Look who decided to show up. Thought you'd crawl away and die, did you?"

Jace's eyes blazed with fury. "You're gonna pay for what you did, Rico. You and your boys."

Rico laughed, a harsh, grating sound. "Big words for a man who's about to die. Take them out, boys."

Chaos erupted as gunfire filled the air. Mari ducked behind a crate, firing at the nearest enemy. Bullets whizzed past her, the sound deafening. She caught a glimpse of Jace, his movements swift and deadly, taking out anyone who crossed his path.

Mari's heart raced as she fought alongside Jace and his crew. She felt a surge of adrenaline, her fear giving way to determination. She couldn't let them down, couldn't let Jace down.

Suddenly, a figure appeared out of nowhere, grabbing her from behind. Mari struggled, but the grip was too strong. She felt a cold barrel pressed against her temple.

"Drop your gun, or she dies," the man growled.

Jace froze, his eyes locking onto Mari's. "Let her go, and I'll drop it."

"Don't do it, Jace," Mari pleaded, her voice trembling. "Take him out."

Jace's jaw clenched, but he didn't move. The man smirked, tightening his grip on Mari. "Smart choice. Now, throw the gun away."

Jace complied, tossing his gun to the side. The man laughed, but his victory was short-lived. One of Jace's allies appeared behind him, delivering a swift blow to the head. The man crumpled, releasing Mari.

"Thanks," Mari gasped, retrieving her gun.

"Don't mention it," the ally replied, before diving back into the fray.

The battle raged on, the air thick with smoke and the smell of gunpowder. Mari and Jace fought side by side, their movements synchronized. The bond between them was unbreakable, forged in the heat of battle.

Finally, the gunfire ceased, the warehouse falling silent. Rico lay on the ground, clutching a bullet wound in his side. Jace stood over him, his expression hard.

"It's over, Rico," Jace said coldly. "You're done."

Rico laughed weakly, blood bubbling from his lips. "You think this ends with me? There's always someone else. You'll never be free."

Jace's eyes darkened, but he didn't respond. He turned away, pulling Mari into his arms. "You okay?"

Mari nodded, her body trembling. "Yeah, I'm fine. We did it."

Jace's crew gathered around, their expressions a mix of relief and exhaustion. They had won, but the cost had been high. Lives had been lost, and the danger was far from over.

As they left the warehouse, the first light of dawn breaking on the horizon, Mari felt a sense of resolve. She had proven her loyalty and bravery, but she knew their fight was far from over. They would have to stay vigilant, ready for whatever came next.

Chapter 14: New Alliances

Jace and Mari sat in a dimly lit room, their breaths heavy with exhaustion. The recent confrontation had left them battered, but not broken. As they looked around at the remaining members of their crew, a sense of determination filled the air. They had survived the onslaught, but they knew that to truly escape the dangers of the drug game, they needed stronger allies.

"We can't keep doin' this," Jace said, his voice low but firm. "We gotta find a way out, and we can't do it alone."

Mari nodded, her eyes steely with resolve. "Who do we trust?"

Jace leaned back, considering his options. "There's a couple of folks I know. They ain't exactly saints, but they got connections. If we can get them on our side, we might have a shot."

They spent the next few days reaching out to potential allies, setting up meetings in discreet locations. One by one, they met with old friends, former rivals, and anyone who could offer them a way out. The conversations were tense, filled with distrust and suspicion, but slowly, they began to forge new alliances.

In a run-down bar on the outskirts of town, Jace and Mari met with Big Tony, a notorious figure with a reputation for getting things done. He was a large man with a presence that demanded respect, and as he approached their table, the room seemed to grow quieter.

"Jace," Big Tony said, his voice a deep rumble. "I heard you got yourself in some deep shit."

Jace nodded, his expression serious. "We need your help, Tony. We wanna get outta the game. Start fresh."

Big Tony leaned back, eyeing them both carefully. "That ain't easy, you know. People don't just walk away from this life."

"We're not lookin' for easy," Mari interjected, her tone fierce. "We're lookin' for a way to survive. We got plans, but we need allies."

Tony looked at her, a smirk playing at the corner of his mouth. "You got fire, girl. I like that. But you gotta understand, helpin' you ain't just a favor. It's an investment."

Jace glanced at Mari before turning back to Tony. "We know. And we're willin' to make it worth your while."

They spent hours negotiating, outlining their plans and how Tony could benefit. By the end of the meeting, an agreement was reached. Tony would provide them with the resources and protection they needed, in exchange for a share in their future ventures.

As they left the bar, Mari felt a glimmer of hope. They had taken the first step towards a new life, but she knew there was still much to do.

Back at their safe house, Mari sat down with Jace, her laptop open in front of her. "I've been thinking," she said, her voice tentative. "About my social media. I've been hiding the truth from my followers, but maybe it's time I show them the real me."

Jace raised an eyebrow. "You sure about that? Once you put it out there, you can't take it back."

Mari nodded. "I'm sure. If we're gonna start over, I need to be honest. With myself, and with them."

She spent the next few days crafting a new approach to her online presence. Instead of the polished, perfect life she had shown before, she started sharing glimpses of her real experiences. The struggles, the danger, the love she had found in the most unexpected place.

Her first post was a simple picture of her and Jace, standing together amidst the chaos of their recent battle. The caption read, "Life ain't always what it seems. Sometimes, the hardest roads lead to the most beautiful destinations. #Truth #NewBeginnings"

The response was immediate and overwhelming. Her followers were shocked, intrigued, and supportive. They wanted to know more, to understand the journey she had been on. Mari found herself flooded with messages, both positive and negative, but she stayed true to her decision to be authentic.

As the days turned into weeks, Mari and Jace continued to build their new life. They used their alliances to dismantle the remnants of their old world, piece by piece. They sold off assets, cut ties with dangerous connections, and planned for a future where they could live without fear.

One evening, as they sat on the porch of their new, modest home, Mari looked at Jace, a smile playing on her lips. "We did it," she said softly. "We're really doing it."

Jace wrapped an arm around her, pulling her close. "Yeah, we are. But we gotta stay sharp. This ain't over yet."

Mari nodded, understanding the reality of their situation. But for the first time in a long while, she felt a sense of peace. They had come a long way, and while the road ahead was still uncertain, they were ready to face it together.

Chapter 15: A Clean Slate

Mari and Jace drove through the winding roads of their new city, the skyline rising in the distance. It was a world away from the grime and danger they had left behind. The move was both exhilarating and daunting. They were here to start fresh, to build a life free from the shadows of their past.

Jace glanced at Mari, her eyes filled with a mix of hope and apprehension. "You ready for this?"

Mari smiled, though her heart raced with uncertainty. "As ready as I'll ever be. It's time for a new beginning."

They pulled up to their new home, a modest house in a quiet neighborhood. It was a far cry from the hustle and bustle they were used to, but that was precisely the point. They needed a place where they could breathe, where they could plan their future without constantly looking over their shoulders.

Inside, the house was bare, the rooms echoing with the promise of what could be. Jace set down the last of their boxes, wiping sweat from his brow. "We gonna make this place ours, Mari. I can feel it."

Mari nodded, her eyes scanning the empty space. "Yeah, we will. But it's gonna take some getting used to."

Their first night in the new house was surreal. The silence was almost deafening after the constant noise and chaos of their previous life. As they lay in bed, Mari turned to Jace, her voice barely a whisper. "Do you ever think about it? The life we left behind?"

Jace sighed, staring at the ceiling. "Every day. But we can't go back. We gotta focus on what's ahead."

The next morning, they set to work on their new venture. They had decided to open a small café, a place where people could come and relax, far removed from the dark world they had escaped. Mari threw herself into the business, her social media skills proving invaluable in promoting their new endeavor.

"Good morning, y'all! It's Mari, and I'm excited to share our new adventure with you. We're opening a café right here in this beautiful city. Come check us out, and let's make some new memories together!" she posted, her enthusiasm genuine.

The response was immediate. Her followers, intrigued by her authenticity, flocked to the café. Business boomed, and for a while, it seemed like they had truly left their past behind.

But adjusting to a normal life was harder than they had anticipated. The café was a success, but the ghosts of their past still lingered. Jace struggled with the mundanity of everyday tasks, the adrenaline of his former life replaced by the steady grind of business ownership.

One evening, as they were closing up, Jace slammed a stack of bills on the counter. "This ain't enough, Mari. We're barely scraping by."

Mari looked up from her paperwork, frustration etched on her face. "What did you expect, Jace? This is how normal people live. We don't have to worry about getting shot or arrested. Isn't that worth something?"

Jace ran a hand through his hair, exhaling sharply. "I know. It's just... I ain't used to this. It's hard."

Mari softened, walking over to him. "We'll get through it. Together. We just have to be patient."

But patience was something they both struggled with. The transition from chaos to calm was jarring, and their past had a way of creeping into their present. Jace had nightmares, reliving the violence and betrayal. Mari found it hard to reconcile the gritty reality they had left behind with the peaceful life they were trying to build.

One night, as they sat on their porch, Mari turned to Jace, her eyes filled with determination. "We can't keep letting the past haunt us. We have to let it go."

Jace nodded, his jaw clenched. "I'm trying, Mari. I really am."

"I know," she said softly, taking his hand. "But we have to do this together. We have to support each other."

Their struggle was far from over, but they were committed to making it work. They poured their hearts into the café, slowly but surely finding joy in the small victories. They built relationships with their customers, finding solace in the community they were creating.

Mari continued to share their journey online, her posts raw and real. "Life ain't always easy, but it's the hard times that make us appreciate the good. We're building something new here, and it's worth every struggle."

As the months passed, they began to settle into their new life. The café flourished, and they found a rhythm in their daily routine. The nightmares became less frequent, the memories of their past fading into the background.

One day, as they sat together in the café, watching the customers enjoy their coffee, Mari turned to Jace, a smile spreading across her face. "We did it, Jace. We really did it."

Jace nodded, his eyes shining with pride. "Yeah, we did. And we'll keep doing it. Every day."

Chapter 16: Facing Demons

Mari sat on the porch of their modest home, staring out into the night. The café had closed for the day, and the quiet was almost unsettling. Jace was inside, dealing with his own ghosts. It had been months since they left their old lives behind, but the past had a way of creeping back, gnawing at their peace.

"Yo, you okay out here?" Jace's voice broke through her thoughts. He stepped onto the porch, a bottle of beer in hand. His eyes were weary, but there was a spark of concern for her.

"I'm fine, Jace," Mari replied, though her voice lacked conviction. "Just thinking about everything."

Jace sat down beside her, taking a swig of his beer. "Yeah, me too. It's hard to shake off, you know? All the shit we went through."

Mari nodded, a heavy silence settling between them. "I've been having these dreams," she admitted, her voice barely a whisper. "About the things we've done, the people we've hurt. It's like they're haunting me."

Jace sighed, placing a comforting arm around her. "Me too. I see their faces every night. But we gotta move forward, Mari. We can't let the past control us."

She looked at him, tears glistening in her eyes. "How do we do that, Jace? How do we find peace?"

Jace pulled her closer, his voice soft yet firm. "We face it. We confront those demons head-on, together."

The next morning, they decided to visit the graves of Jace's fallen comrades, people who had died because of their lifestyle. It was a pilgrimage of sorts, a way to pay respects and seek forgiveness. The cemetery was eerily quiet, the gravestones standing like silent sentinels.

Jace knelt beside one of the graves, his expression pained. "This is where it started, Mari. The choices, the bloodshed. We owe it to them to make things right."

Mari placed a hand on his shoulder, feeling his pain as if it were her own. "We do, Jace. And we will."

They spent hours at the cemetery, each grave a stark reminder of their past. They talked about the memories, the regrets, and the moments that had led them to where they were now. It was a cathartic experience, the weight of their guilt slowly lifting.

That evening, they returned home, exhausted but lighter. They sat on the porch once again, the night air cool and soothing.

"I think we took the first step today," Mari said, her voice filled with a newfound resolve. "But there's still more to do."

Jace nodded, his gaze distant. "I know. There's people I need to make amends with, things I need to set right."

Mari took his hand, squeezing it gently. "We'll do it together. No matter how hard it gets."

The following weeks were a whirlwind of confrontations and reconciliations. Jace reached out to old friends and former enemies, seeking forgiveness and offering apologies. It wasn't easy, and some meetings ended in heated arguments, but it was a necessary process.

Mari, too, faced her demons. She began attending therapy, confronting the trauma and guilt that had plagued her for so long. She shared her experiences with her followers, her honesty resonating with many who had faced similar struggles.

"Hey everyone," she posted one evening. "Life ain't always perfect, and we all have our demons. But facing them is the first step towards healing. Let's do this together. #Healing #Truth"

The response was overwhelming. Messages of support and shared experiences flooded her inbox. It was a reminder that she wasn't alone, that they weren't alone.

One night, after a particularly intense therapy session, Mari found Jace in their bedroom, staring at an old photograph. It was a picture of him and his best friend, both of them smiling, full of life.

"Who's that?" she asked, sitting beside him.

Jace sighed, his voice heavy with emotion. "His name was Darnell. We were like brothers. He died because of me, because of my choices."

Mari wrapped her arms around him, offering comfort. "You can't blame yourself forever, Jace. You've changed. We've changed."

He nodded, tears streaming down his face. "I know. But it still hurts."

They sat in silence, the weight of their shared pain a bond that only strengthened their relationship. They had faced their demons, but the road to healing was long and arduous.

As the weeks turned into months, they continued to support each other through the emotional turmoil. Their love grew stronger, their bond unbreakable. They found peace in the small moments, the quiet evenings spent together, the laughter they shared.

One evening, as they sat on the porch, Mari turned to Jace, her eyes filled with gratitude. "We've come a long way, haven't we?"

Jace smiled, his eyes reflecting the same gratitude. "Yeah, we have. And we'll keep moving forward. Together."

Chapter 17: A New Beginning

Mari and Jace stood on the balcony of their modest home, gazing out at the city that had become their refuge. The sun was setting, casting a golden hue over the skyline, a stark contrast to the chaos that once ruled their lives. The journey they had been on was nothing short of tumultuous, but standing there together, they felt a profound sense of peace.

Jace wrapped his arm around Mari, pulling her close. "We've come a long way, huh?" he said, his voice soft but filled with emotion.

Mari nodded, leaning her head on his shoulder. "Yeah, we have. And I wouldn't change a thing. Everything we went through brought us here."

They had spent months rebuilding their lives, facing their past demons, and forging a new path together. The café they had opened was thriving, a symbol of their resilience and determination. It wasn't just a business; it was a testament to their journey, a place where they could start anew.

Despite the peace they had found, the gritty reality of their past was never far behind. They had made powerful enemies, and the streets they had once ruled were still fraught with danger. But Mari and Jace had learned to navigate these challenges, their bond growing stronger with each passing day.

One evening, as they were closing up the café, a familiar face walked through the door. It was Big Tony, the man who had once helped them secure their escape from the drug game. He was a large, imposing figure, but his eyes held a warmth that belied his tough exterior.

"Yo, Jace, Mari," he greeted, his deep voice resonating through the café. "Heard y'all been doin' good. Mind if I sit?"

Jace nodded, pulling out a chair. "Sure thing, Tony. What brings you here?"

Tony sat down, his expression serious. "I been hearin' things. Word on the street is some of your old enemies are lookin' for payback. Thought you should know."

Mari's heart skipped a beat, but she kept her composure. "Thanks for the heads up, Tony. We knew this might happen."

Jace leaned forward, his eyes narrowing. "What do you know?"

Tony sighed, rubbing his temples. "There's talk about a hit. Some folks ain't happy you just walked away. They see your success, and they're jealous. Figured I'd warn you, outta respect."

Mari and Jace exchanged a look, the gravity of the situation sinking in. They had worked so hard to leave their past behind, but it seemed the past wasn't done with them yet.

"Thanks, Tony," Jace said, his voice tense. "We appreciate it."

Tony nodded, standing up. "Take care of yourselves. And watch your backs."

As Tony left, Mari felt a surge of anxiety. "What are we gonna do, Jace?"

Jace took a deep breath, his jaw set in determination. "We ain't gonna let them scare us. We built this life, and we're gonna protect it. Together."

The next few weeks were a whirlwind of preparation. They increased security at the café, installed cameras around their home, and made sure they were always aware of their surroundings. It was a stressful time, but Mari and Jace faced it head-on, their bond only strengthening in the face of adversity.

One night, as they were locking up the café, a car pulled up to the curb. Mari's heart raced as she saw a group of men step out, their intentions clear.

"Stay behind me," Jace whispered, his hand moving to the gun he kept hidden under the counter.

The men approached, their leader stepping forward. "We need to talk," he said, his voice cold and menacing.

Jace stood his ground, his eyes locked on the leader. "We ain't got nothin' to say to you."

The leader smirked, his hand resting on the gun tucked into his waistband. "See, that's where you're wrong. You owe us. And we're here to collect."

Mari's breath caught in her throat, but she refused to show fear. "We left that life behind. We're not going back."

The leader's smirk turned into a sneer. "You think you can just walk away? There's a price for everything."

Before he could draw his weapon, Jace moved swiftly, his gun aimed at the leader's chest. "I suggest you leave. Now."

The tension was palpable, the air thick with the promise of violence. For a moment, it seemed like a shootout was inevitable. But the leader hesitated, realizing the odds were not in his favor.

"Fine," he spat, signaling his men to back off. "But this ain't over. We'll be back."

As they drove away, Mari let out a shaky breath. "That was too close."

Jace nodded, his eyes still locked on the retreating car. "Yeah. But we handled it. We'll always handle it."

Despite the threats, they refused to live in fear. They continued to build their life, each day a testament to their resilience. The café became a haven, not just for them, but for the community. It was a place where people could escape the harsh realities of the streets, if only for a little while.

Mari's social media presence continued to grow, her followers inspired by her authenticity and strength. She shared their journey, the struggles and triumphs, always keeping it real.

"Life ain't always easy," she posted one day. "But it's the hard times that make us appreciate the good. We've faced our demons, and we've come out stronger. Thank y'all for being part of this journey with us. #NewBeginnings #StayStrong"

The response was overwhelming. Messages of support and admiration poured in, reminding Mari that they were not alone. They had a community, both online and in real life, that believed in them.

One evening, as they sat on their porch, Mari turned to Jace, a smile playing on her lips. "We did it, Jace. We built a life worth living."

Jace nodded, his eyes filled with pride. "Yeah, we did. And we'll keep building it. Together."

Their journey had been long and arduous, filled with danger and heartbreak. But standing there, with the city lights twinkling in the distance, they knew they had found something priceless. They had found each other, and that was worth more than anything else.

As the night wore on, they talked about their future, their dreams and plans. They wanted to expand the café, to create a space where people could come and find solace. They dreamed of traveling, of seeing the world together. And most importantly, they dreamed of a family, of raising children in a world they had fought so hard to create.

"We've come a long way," Jace said, his voice soft. "And we got a long way to go. But I'm ready for it. With you."

Mari's heart swelled with love and gratitude. "Me too, Jace. Me too."

Don't miss out!

Visit the website below and you can sign up to receive emails whenever Rachael Reed publishes a new book. There's no charge and no obligation.

https://books2read.com/r/B-A-WXARB-OQJVD

BOOKS 2 READ

Connecting independent readers to independent writers.

Did you love *Link in Bio*? Then you should read *Backpage Hustle*[1] by Rachael Reed!

[2]

Theresa "Sugar" Graham was born into a world where the streets don't play fair, and neither does she. Hustlin' on Backpage, she's clawed her way from nothin' to somethin', usin' her beauty, brains, and cold-blooded ambition to climb to the top. But when she meets Derrick "Big D" Poindexter, an old-school pimp with a twisted sense of loyalty, her life takes a dark and dangerous turn.

With Big D's connections and her street smarts, Sugar quickly transforms from a project chick to the Hood Queen. She's got money, power, and respect, but in the game of survival, there's always someone lookin' to take what you got. As jealousy and betrayal swirl around her,

---

1. https://books2read.com/u/3GlLy8

2. https://books2read.com/u/3GlLy8

Sugar must navigate a world of deceit, violence, and lust. Enemies lurk in every shadow, and trust is a luxury she can't afford.

When an unexpected betrayal leads to a bloody showdown, Sugar's world is shattered. Locked up and fighting for survival behind bars, she plots her revenge, determined to reclaim her throne and take down Big D once and for all. But the streets don't forget, and neither does Sugar.

Back on the outside, she's ready to unleash a storm of vengeance. Allies turn enemies, and the line between right and wrong blurs in a deadly game of power and survival. As the body count rises and the stakes get higher, Sugar faces her ultimate test. Can she break free from the cycle of violence and chaos, or will the streets consume her for good?

Backpage Hustle is a gripping, heart-pounding urban drama that dives deep into the gritty underworld of city life. With raw, streetwise dialogue and a cast of unforgettable characters, this tale of ambition, betrayal, and revenge will keep you on the edge of your seat. Get ready for a wild ride through the dark side of the city, where every choice could be your last, and only the strongest survive.

Also by Rachael Reed

Codefendant
Codefendant
Once a Cheater
Once a Cheater
Passport Bro
What Happens in Prison
Preference
Sprinkle Sprinkle
Championship Bad
Street Exodus
Street Exodus
Street Royalty
Pawns of Power
SIS
Cartel Bloodline
Get Money Girls
Skip the Games
Til Death Do Us Part
Backpage Hustle
Link in Bio